Ellie's Magical Bakery

Best Cake for a Best Friend

ELLIE SIMMONDS

Illustrated by Kimberley Scott

RED FOX

Greyton
Woods and
Waterfall

Abandoned
Shop

Greyton
Green

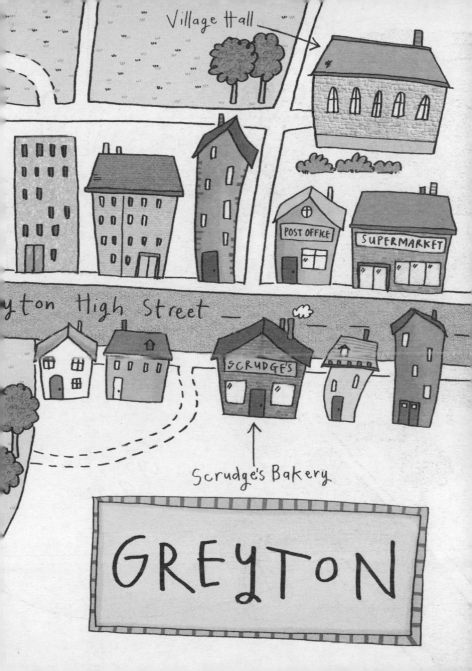

Chapter 1

It was the morning of Ellie's birthday. Before she stepped into Scrudge's Bakery she took a deep breath to give herself courage . . . then wished she hadn't. The bakery smelled like old socks and soggy cabbage. *Revolting, as usual*, Ellie thought.

She looked around the bakery, hoping she might have a birthday present. The shelves were lined with week-old bread,

stale, stodgy cakes and mouldy muffins. Her uncle, Mr Scrudge, stood behind one of the shop counters mixing cookie dough. Ellie watched as he shoved a fistful of chocolate chips into his mouth, then swept a handful of dead flies off the worktop and into the dough. *Yuck!*

And there was no sign of a present.

Ellie knew very little about her mum, and her dad had died three years ago. She remembered his ginger beard, round cheeks and silly deep chuckle. Whenever she thought about him she was surrounded by the aroma of freshly baked cakes . . . not this horrible smell! Her aunt and uncle ran her father's bakery now.

They had changed the name of the shop to 'Scrudge's Bakery' and had moved into the flat above it with Ellie and her ginger cat, Whisk.

She hadn't had a birthday present since.

Mrs Scrudge was slouching in a chair behind the till, her belly squeezing out of the top of her trousers. "What do *you* want, Shrimp?" she asked Ellie, straining to reach a mug of tea.

Ellie passed her the mug. There *was* something she wanted – even more than a present. She was going

to ask her aunt and uncle
for a special birthday treat.

Whisk ran over and
rubbed up against her leg.
It gave her courage.

"Umm, it's my birth—"
she started to say.

But the door to the shop suddenly
opened and a man walked in.

"Customers! Quiet!" hissed Mrs Scrudge,
and heaved herself up in her chair.

Whisk hissed. Ellie stroked his fur and
looked up to see who it was. Customers
were rare since the Scrudges had taken
over the bakery. It was Mr Amrit,

a man she'd seen around the village. Clearly he hadn't heard how awful the food was here.

He strode up to the counter confidently, then caught sight of the horrible-looking cakes, cringed, and held his nose.

"Hello, sir," Mrs Scrudge simpered, batting her eyelashes. "Do buy something from our delightful shop."

"Er . . . no thank you," said Mr Amrit, backing out of the door. "I've just remembered, I . . ."

Ellie went to hold the door for him – she couldn't blame Mr Amrit for wanting to leave. But her aunt lunged forward

6

and grabbed Ellie's arm while her uncle blocked poor Mr Amrit's exit. Mr Scrudge was huge – the size of a garden shed – with stubble on his face and neck.

"Buy something from our delightful shop," he growled. "Or else!" He put up his fist.

Mr Amrit cowered, then forced a smile onto his face. "My wife *is* partial to carrot cake," he said, his voice shaking with fear. "D-d-do you have some?"

Mrs Scrudge gave him a slice of cake. It was furrier than Whisk.

"Do you think that's safe to eat?" Ellie asked her aunt. "It looks a bit green."

"'Course it's green," Mrs Scrudge snapped. "It's Brussels sprout cake."

Ellie winced.

Mr Amrit winced.

Even Whisk winced.

Who would want to eat a Brussels sprout cake?

"It was *carrot* cake I was after," Mr Amrit said. "You know, with the creamy white icing—'

Mr Scrudge raised his fists again and Mr Amrit said, "But this looks nice too." He took the cake, handed over his money and hurried out of the shop.

"Come back soon!" called Mrs Scrudge, then she slumped back in her chair, puffing from the effort.

Ellie felt terribly sorry for Mr Amrit. Cakes were supposed to be delicious, tasty treats. The Scrudges' definitely weren't.

She'd never dared eat any of their cakes
– not since she'd heard worrying gurgly
noises coming from the tummies of the
villagers who had. But when Ellie was
younger, her dad had let her help in the

bakery. She wanted to
try baking again – to
make her very own
birthday cake.

"Uncle," she said.
"It's my birth—"

"I'm busy!" he yelled
at her. But he was only
busy cleaning out his
ears with his finger.

10

"I could help you in the bakery if you like." Ellie pulled her long brown hair into a ponytail, ready to get stuck in.

Mr Scrudge turned and laughed. "Don't be ridiculous!"

Mrs Scrudge laughed too. "You are too small and too stupid to make cakes. In fact, you're too small and too stupid to do anything."

Ellie crossed her arms in front of her chest. She *was* small. She had a condition called achondroplasia, which meant she was shorter than most people.

But there was no such thing as *too small*. An ant can lift things fifty times heavier than itself. A salmon swims thousands of miles. Even the smallest birthday present can make a person very happy.

And Ellie was most certainly *not* stupid.

"But if you would like to prove you're not completely useless," Mrs Scrudge said, "go to the garden centre and get me some cement mix. I can't be bothered."

"Why do you need cement mix?" Ellie asked.

"It's cheaper than flour," her aunt replied.

"And mud is cheaper than chocolate," added Mr Scrudge.

Yuck!

"Can't Colin go?" Ellie asked. Colin was her cousin, the Scrudges' twelve-year-old son.

"No," said Mrs Scrudge. "He's out."

Ellie was certain Colin *was* out: he was

13

probably out bullying someone.

"Fine," she said. It was annoying how lazy the Scrudges were, but she was pleased to have an excuse to get away from them.

"Make sure you're back by four," Mr Scrudge called after her. "Or I'll put Whiskers in the next batch!" He threw a burned bun at Ellie's cat.

Whisk miaowed, annoyed.

Ellie snapped back, "My cat's name is *Whisk*!"

"What's a whisk?" said Mrs Scrudge.

Ellie shook her head in dismay – any baker should know what a whisk was!

She held the door open for the cat as they left the shop.

Then she stumbled.

At first she assumed that Colin had left something on the ground on purpose, to trip her up; he'd done that before. But when she looked down, she gasped with surprise. There on the doorstep lay a neatly wrapped present about the size of a pizza box. It had a bow on it, the paper was covered in pictures of cupcakes with candles on, and the words *Happy Birthday Ellie* were written on the front.

"Do you think the Scrudges have bought me a birthday present after all?" Ellie wondered aloud. But deep down she knew that there was more chance of Whisk buying her a present than Mr and Mrs Scrudge.

There was a note on the front that said:

Ellie knew just the place . . .

Chapter 2

Ellie ran down Greyton High Street with the present tucked under her arm, and Whisk following at her heels – she couldn't wait to open it!

The town of Greyton was just like it sounded: the cars were grey; the buildings were grey; even the people looked grey and miserable. Ellie had lived here all her life, but she was sure it hadn't always been like this.

Greyton needed something to sweeten it up. If only she could think of something—

"*Oof!*"

Her present skidded across the ground, along with the boy she'd just knocked over.

"I'm sorry!" they both said at the same time. Ellie picked up his glasses and he picked up her parcel. She pushed back her long brown hair to look at him. She recognized him. He was about her age, and every time she saw him around the village

he was wearing a T-shirt with a different animal on it.

Today's T-shirt had a tiger on. Whisk purred at it.

"I didn't see you because I was looking at the notice board," he said.

Ellie followed the boy's eyes to the village notice board next to him. A poster pinned to it read:

Are you a budding baker?

Why not enter

THE GREYTON BAKE-OFF?

♡ Sunday at midday ♡

Let the best baker win!

Every year the bake-off was held on the village green. It wasn't as lovely as it sounded. In Greyton, even the green was grey.

"Are you going to enter?" Ellie asked the boy.

He looked from left to right, as if he was scared to talk to her.

This often happened. Ellie's achrondroplasia meant that her arms and legs were shorter than a lot of people's. She didn't mind being small, and she didn't mind being different, but she had no friends — and that she *did* mind. Now that her dad was gone, Ellie felt very lonely.

Finally the boy said, "My cakes *taste* good even if they don't *look* perfect. But it doesn't matter anyway – the Scrudges always win the bake-off so there is no point entering."

Every year the Scrudges threatened people to stop them from taking part.

"Well, the Scrudges *are* the best bakers in the competition," said Ellie with a sad chuckle. "Because they are the *only* bakers in the competition."

The boy laughed. "I'm Basil," he said, "and—" He stopped.

Ellie saw who Basil was looking at and her heart sank. Her cousin, Colin, his hair sticky with bits of food.

Colin was older than Ellie, twice as mean as his parents, and three times as tubby.

"Why are you talking to *her*?" he shouted as he stomped over; he towered over Basil. "She's so small and stupid. Are you stupid too, Basil?"

22

From the way Basil was gulping, Ellie
could tell he was trying not to cry.

She moved next to Basil and it made her
feel braver. "Stop being a bully, Colin,"
she said.

"Who said that?" Colin sneered. "Oh,
didn't see you there, Ellie."

She walked forward so she was standing right opposite him. She only came up to his chest, but for once she wasn't scared. "Pick on someone your own size!"

"The only thing the same size as you is a tiny little ant," he said.

Ellie knew that ants were strong and it made her feel strong too. "The only thing the same size as your brain is an ant's fingernail."

"Ants don't have fingernails," Colin replied.

"Exactly!" she said.

"Well, you are . . . I . . . erm . . ." Colin didn't know what to say to that. He looked back and forth between Basil and Ellie. "I'll get you, Ellie," he said. Then he ran off.

Basil sniffed as Whisk rubbed up against his leg to comfort him. "That was brave," he said.

"If we stick together," Ellie replied, "we can all be brave." It's what her dad had said when he'd given her Whisk.

Whisk was a good cat, but he couldn't stand up for her when Colin and the Scrudges were picking on her, calling

her "stupid" and "small".

"See you around . . ." Ellie was about to leave, but she wondered if she could be even braver with a friend by her side. "I'm going to my favourite place to open my birthday present."

Basil's face lit up. "Is it your birthday today?" he asked.

"Yes." For a moment Ellie worried about trusting Basil, but she'd never make any friends if she didn't try. "I'll show you if you promise to keep it a secret."

Basil nodded. "I promise," he said. He didn't seem scared of being seen with her any more.

"Happy birthday," he added, and they headed off into the woods.

Chapter 3

Ellie's secret spot was a secluded clearing in the nearby woods. There was a small waterfall trickling down a rocky slope, where the water gathered in a clear pool. It was only minutes from the high street, but the miserable people of Greyton never went walking in the woods.

"Wowweee!" said Basil. "What a cool place. I had no idea it was here."

"I come here to swim," Ellie told him. "I love swimming."

They sat side by side on a log that faced the pool. Whisk padded about at their feet.

Ellie took a deep breath. "Here goes!" She ripped off the paper really quickly, not caring about spoiling the wrapping.

Inside was a big thick hardback book. On the front was a picture of a cupcake with mounds of yummy-looking white icing. As Ellie pulled off the last of the paper, a puff of glitter flew up into the air.

The title of the book was:

Victoria Sponge's
Magical Recipe Book

Ellie's heart was racing. Who had sent it? What was a magical recipe book? There was only one way to find out . . .

But when Ellie opened the book, the pages were blank.

"Oh." Ellie tried to hide her disappointment. What use was a recipe book with no recipes in it? Perhaps Colin was playing a trick on her, after all.

"Wait! What's this?" said Basil. He bent down and picked up a piece of paper from the ground. It was about the size of postcard. "This must have fallen out." He handed it to Ellie.

Ellie's hand shook as she held the card.

Dear Ellie,

   I hope this message gets to you on your birthday. There is magic everywhere, but especially inside this book. I love you very much and wish I was still with you. But I've got you a present, and I have asked a good friend of mine to help you with it . . .

      Love from

        Dad

Ellie remembered her father's ginger beard and silly, deep chuckle. And the aroma of freshly baked cakes. He must have left this present with somebody before he died. She tried to hide her tears.

"Do you think it really *is* magic?" asked Basil.

As he spoke, something started moving, like worms wriggling across the page. Ellie blinked, wondering if her teary eyes were playing tricks on her. But they weren't worms, they were *words*. The book was writing itself.

"It *is* magic!" she cried. A picture started to appear – it was a three-layered cake

with candles on top.

Ellie flipped through the book again, and now all the pages were full of cooking instructions and images of mouth-watering treats.

"The recipes don't look too tricky to do," said Basil.

On the very first page there was a drawing of a woman with little golden wings. She looked like a fairy, but instead of a crown, a pretty dress and magic wand, she had a chef's hat, a white apron and wooden spoon.

"Do you think that's Victoria Sponge?" Ellie asked Basil.

As if just saying the words worked some sort of spell, the little baker began to peel out of the book. She flew into the air, leaving a trail of glitter behind her. Whisk jumped up and tried to bat her with his paw like he did when he chased butterflies, but the tiny figure was too fast.

"Did somebody call for me?" Victoria Sponge was the same size as she was on the page – no bigger than Ellie's hand.

Ellie and Basil looked up at the flying baker, too stunned to speak.

"Hello, Ellie," Victoria Sponge said.

Whisk hid behind the log – this was no ordinary butterfly!

"How – how do you know my name?" Ellie managed.

"I knew your father," she replied.

Ellie's mouth dropped open so wide you could fit a hot cross bun in it.

"Your father was an amazing baker," Victoria Sponge continued, hovering around Ellie's head.

"How did you know my dad? Did he put you in this book? Did you cook together? Did you—"

Victoria Sponge laughed. "That's a lot of questions, Ellie!" she said. "The most important thing is that he wanted to arrange a special present for your eighth birthday. He asked me to help him by helping you."

"Wowwee," said Basil.

Ellie looked again at the book and started to read through the recipes. Glittery sugar dust puffed out of the pages as she turned them.

Whisk was curious, and he couldn't

resist jumping up to catch some on his tongue.

Just then, it started raining in big fat drops.

"Oh dear," said Victoria Sponge.

"You'd better get back to the bakery," Basil told Ellie.

"The bakery!" Ellie couldn't believe she'd forgotten the time. It was almost four o'clock, and she still had to buy the cement mix. The Scrudges would be angry.

"Would you . . . ?" Ellie was about to ask the little baker if she would like to shelter in her pocket, but when she turned round Victoria Sponge had disappeared!

Victoria
Sponge's
Magical
Recipe
Book

"Where . . . ?" She looked at the recipe book and saw that Victoria Sponge was back on the first page. The chef in the picture winked at her.

This really *was* a magical birthday! But Mrs Scrudge had said she'd put Whisk in the cake batter if Ellie was late home.

Ellie called goodbye to Basil, and she and Whisk ran out of the woods.

Chapter 4

It was one minute past four when Ellie and Whisk scuttled into the bakery kitchen. She had managed to pick up the cement mix, but it had got heavier and heavier as the rain soaked into it.

"What have you been doing, Shrimp?" grumbled Mrs Scrudge.

The kitchen looked like there had been a party in it since Ellie had left.

There was dirt on the floor and work surfaces. Fingerprints were smeared all over the walls, and even the ceiling!

"What have *you* been doing?" Ellie replied, but her aunt and uncle ignored her.

"I'm going to watch TV," Mr Scrudge said. He took off his apron and dumped

 44

it on top of Whisk.

"For being late and lazy, you have to clean the whole kitchen," added Mrs Scrudge, and she followed Mr Scrudge from the room.

Whisk wriggled out from under the apron, and miaowed in annoyance.

Cleaning the kitchen by herself would

45

take hours, Ellie realized. Then she remembered what Victoria Sponge had said – that Ellie's dad had asked the little baker to help.

She put the magical recipe book down on the worktop and opened it.

"Victoria Sponge?" she whispered. For a moment she wondered if she had imagined the magical creature, but Victoria Sponge popped out of the book in a puff of glittery sugar dust.

"This place is filthy!" The tiny baker waved her wooden spoon crossly

46

in the air. "Dirt here. Muck there. Flies everywhere!"

"You should see what they put in the food," Ellie mumbled.

Victoria Sponge was furious. "Cakes are supposed to be delicious, tasty treats!"

Ellie went to the cupboard under the sink and pulled out some cleaning fluid. Whisk grabbed the dishcloths and sponges with his teeth.

"I'll lend a hand," said Victoria Sponge.

"That's very kind of you," said Ellie. "If I mop the floor" – she started pouring hot water into a bucket – "you could just— Oh!"

When she turned round, the room was clean. So clean it sparkled. The ceiling was smudge-free, the floor was gleaming, the dishes were washed, and even the pans with caked-on food were now shining. Victoria Sponge was wearing rubber gloves, but Ellie doubted she'd used them. This *had* to be magic.

48

"Victoria Sponge, you're amazing! Thank you."

"My pleasure, Ellie," she replied with a smile. "What do you want to do now?"

Ellie thought back to the idea she'd had that morning. "It's still my birthday. I'd really like to bake a birthday cake."

"That's what I hoped you'd say!"

Ellie pulled a chair over to the worktop and stepped up onto it while Victoria Sponge hovered above. Ellie opened the book to the first recipe:

A cake for when you've eaten too much

"I've never heard of a cake like that before," she said.

A perfect pie for a perfect pet

"Are these cakes magical?" Ellie asked. "Did my dad find them?"

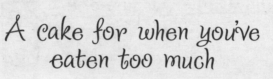

"I don't know,"
said Victoria Sponge
– though Ellie saw a
twinkle in her eye. Victoria Sponge
did know, Ellie was sure of it.

A good night's sleep cake

A cake for a best friend

"If we follow the recipes," said Ellie,
"will the cakes magically make these
things happen?"

"We'll just have to try them and see,"
said Victoria Sponge with a smile.

Ellie turned the page again.

A cake for Ellie's birthday

She wondered if her dad had included this recipe just for today.

"Perfect," said Victoria Sponge.

Ellie got the ingredients together – sugar, eggs, butter, flour (*real* flour, not cement) – and Victoria Sponge helped to measure them out and pour them into the mixing bowl. The little baker broke the first egg, tapping the shell on the side of the bowl, showing Ellie how to do it.

"You have to give it quite a knock," she said.

Eggs were small, but tougher than they looked – just like Ellie.

Whisk watched as Victoria Sponge taught Ellie how to whisk, beating the batch until her arm ached and the batter became light and fluffy.

"It looks yummy!" Ellie said; she couldn't wait for the cake to cook. She wanted to eat it now!

"It will be worth the wait, I promise," said Victoria Sponge. "But you can lick the bowl when we're done."

Ellie remembered her dad saying the exact same thing. "Did you work with my dad in his bakery, then?" she asked.

"What do you think?" the chef replied.

Ellie didn't know what to think any more. It had been a very surprising day!

Victoria Sponge pulled a tub out of her apron pocket.

"What's that?" Ellie asked. She thought they'd included all the ingredients listed in the recipe.

"This is my magical baking dust — it brings out the deliciousness in everything." Victoria Sponge sprinkled a teaspoon of the glittery dust into the bowl.

Now Ellie was even more excited.

Once they had poured the cake mix into a greased tin lined with baking paper, Victoria Sponge helped Ellie put it carefully into the oven. The little baker was stronger than she looked — Ellie had something in common with her there!

They closed the oven door and Ellie leaned her back against it.

"Couldn't you use magic to make the cakes?" Ellie asked.

"Isn't it so much more fun this way?" replied Victoria Sponge, twirling her wooden spoon in the air.

Ellie had to agree. "Making cakes is almost as fun as eating them," she said. "I can't wait to make another one."

"Well," said Victoria Sponge, "why don't we?"

Ellie knew she would be in a lot of trouble if her aunt and uncle found out she was baking. But the cleaning was done, and Victoria Sponge was here to help her. She could hear the Scrudges snoring above the sounds of the television . . .

"Let's do it!" she said.

Ellie and Victoria Sponge made cake after cake after cake: tarts for tea time, cookies for elevenses, birthday cakes for days that aren't your birthday, a cake for a best friend, a cake for a good night's sleep – all with a sprinkling of Victoria Sponge's magical baking dust.

Ellie had to use a lot of will power to stop herself from eating them – she promised she'd wait until they had cooled, and were iced and ready.

Soon the kitchen was full of cakes, cookies and biscuits, pies and pastries of every kind.

Whisk had fallen asleep in an empty box on the floor and was purring quietly. Victoria Sponge floated over and stroked his head.

"What time is it?" Ellie asked her.

As she spoke, an alarm clock went off. They had baked all through the night! Mr and Mrs Scrudge would be downstairs any minute. Ellie knew they would be very angry that she'd made all these cakes without asking. But she wanted to show them that if they made nice food, customers would come without needing to be threatened.

Maybe they could make Scrudge's Bakery the best bakery in the world! Ellie wanted to be brave and face them.

Ellie heard Mr Scrudge's heavy footsteps coming down the stairs.

"Hide!" she shouted to Victoria Sponge, who jumped back into the recipe book.

"Mmmmm," Mr Scrudge said. "Something smells . . ."

Ellie gritted her teeth as she saw the door handle move.

"Shrimp! What are you doing in here?" Mr Scrudge yelled.

Mrs Scrudge appeared by his side,

scowling. "How many times have we told you? You are too small and too stupid to make cakes! You're too small and too stupid to do anything."

Ellie felt a little scared. But as she looked around at the mountains of yummy food, she also felt more sure than ever that she *wasn't* too small or too stupid to do anything.

She looked her uncle in the eye.

"Why don't you try one?" she asked.

Chapter 5

Mr Scrudge dipped his grimy finger into one of Ellie's cupcakes, scooped up a dollop of the lavender icing, and looked at it as if it might poison him.

Ellie stood with her hands on her hips. She hadn't actually tasted any of the cakes herself yet, but they smelled lovely. And Victoria Sponge had said that her magical baking dust brought out the

deliciousness in everything.

Mr Scrudge winced as he put his finger in his mouth.

Ellie winced as she waited for his reaction.

Whisk winced, just to join in.

First one bushy eyebrow lifted, then another . . . Her uncle's eyes widened in excitement. Eventually he couldn't help himself. "It's delicious!" he said, smiling.

Ellie didn't think she had ever seen him smile before.

He took another scoop of the icing, and ate it.

Mrs Scrudge grabbed a cupcake and took a bite.

"How does it taste?" Ellie asked nervously.

"Mmm–mmm–m–m–mmm," her aunt replied, which Ellie took as a good sign. Mrs Scrudge's eyes turned to all the other cakes and biscuits in the room. Normally she didn't like to move very much, but now she walked around the room, grabbing handfuls of food and shoving it in her mouth. Mr Scrudge joined in, pushing past his wife to get there first.

They ate more and more without swallowing.

"Slow down," said Ellie. "You'll get indigestion!"

What would happen to the magic in the cakes if the Scrudges ate them all? Ellie didn't know if the magic even worked.

"Wait," she begged. "We could sell them in the shop. We could make Scrudge's

Bakery the best—"

"I can't be bothered," said Mrs Scrudge. "We'll sell the ones that are already on the shelf."

The ones that had been there for months.

"These cakes are too good for the idiots of Greyton." Mr Scrudge spat crumbs everywhere as he spoke.

The kitchen door opened and Colin walked in.

"Just in time, darling," Mrs Scrudge told him. "Ellie bought these cakes. Help me stuff them into my mouth."

"I'm not helping you," Colin said to his mother. "Why would I, when *I* want them?" He ran over and started munching too.

"I didn't *buy* them," Ellie insisted, "I made them."

"Liar," said her uncle.

Ellie hadn't eaten any of her own birthday cake. She had no idea what kind of magic it would perform, but she wanted to find out. From the way Whisk had stared at it, Ellie knew he wanted some too. She also thought Basil might like a slice.

"Oh, look, this one's got icing on it!" Colin shouted. "*Happy Birthday Ellie.* I don't know anyone by that name." He sneered at her. "But *I've* got a birthday this year. Must mean it's for me."

His parents laughed.

"Can I have a little, please?" Ellie asked.

Whisk miaowed – which was his way of asking politely.

But Colin stuffed slice after slice into his mouth. "Thorry. All gwone."

Ellie shook her head in dismay.

Colin gave a big yawn. As he did so, a button popped off and he had to catch his trousers before they fell down! "I think I'll just sit down for a minute," he said.

"Me too," said Mr Scrudge.

"I need a rest as well," said Mrs Scrudge, who spent more time *resting* than actually *doing* every day.

Before long they were all snoring; clumps of cake fell out of their hands and onto the floor.

Ellie felt sleepy because she'd been awake all night — but what was their excuse? Then she remembered that one of the cakes was *A good night's sleep cake*. Had the Scrudges just eaten too much or was this Victoria Sponge's magic working?

Whisk rubbed up against Ellie. "Oh, Whisk," she said as she stroked his ginger ears. "The Scrudges have no interest in

73

running a nice bakery with nice cakes and nice ingredients. I wish *I* could start my own bakery – making delicious things for the people of Greyton." Ellie thought back to Mr Amrit trying to buy a carrot cake for his wife. "But the Scrudges think I am too small and too stupid."

"There's no such thing as *too small*!"

Ellie jumped. Whisk jumped too. Victoria Sponge had reappeared in a puff of glittery sugar dust.

"*I'm small*," she said, "and it's never stopped me doing anything!"

"But how do I *prove* that I am a real baker—?" Suddenly Ellie remembered the poster she and Basil had seen yesterday. "The bake-off!" If she won the Greyton village bake-off, she'd show the Scrudges that she could make cakes as well as anyone. Then maybe they'd let her sell her cakes in their shop . . .

"That's a brilliant idea!" Victoria Sponge twirled around Ellie's head, making Ellie's long brown hair fly up.

But the bake-off started at midday. The Scrudges had eaten all her cakes and there wasn't enough time to make another one.

"The cakes are all gone," Ellie said, her voice sounding as heavy as her heart felt.

"Maybe not . . ." said Victoria Sponge, with a twinkle in her eye. "I might have managed to hide one."

Ellie hadn't seen Victoria hide any, and she'd been here the whole time. But then she remembered how the magical baker had cleaned the kitchen in the blink of an eye. She could have hidden a cake just as quickly.

The Scrudges were still snoring, their faces covered in food. Victoria Sponge winked at Ellie, flapped her golden wings, flew up to the highest shelf and brought down a cake.

76

A cake for a best friend

"Yesssss!" cried Ellie, then slapped her hand over her mouth. Luckily the Scrudges didn't move. Could it be magic, after all? They had a cake.

"But where can we go to ice it?" Ellie wondered aloud. "I don't want to be here when the Scrudges wake up."

"Don't worry," Victoria Sponge whispered. "I know just the place."

Chapter 6

Ellie stared at the smallest shop on the high street. It was tiny – about the size of a playhouse – with a small door and a counter at the front that meant you could serve people directly from the pavement. Ellie had seen the shop before and had always wondered about it. Anyone else would have had to crouch to get in, but not Ellie. It was the perfect size for her. The shop was boarded up — it had been for as long as she could remember. She looked up at the sign above the door, but the letters were too faded to make out.

"What kind of shop do you think this was?" she asked Whisk.

"Miaow," Whisk replied, which wasn't much of an answer.

Victoria Sponge pointed her wooden spoon at a loose board and Ellie pulled it back as far as she could. It was a tight squeeze for Ellie, Victoria Sponge and Whisk to fit through, but sometimes being small had its benefits! They wriggled inside.

Ellie gasped when she looked around the shop.

It was a bakery kitchen, but unlike any she'd ever imagined. There were three ovens: one that was the right size for tiny Victoria Sponge to use; one that was the right size for Ellie to use;

and one that was the same size as the one in the Scrudges' kitchen. There were three different-sized worktops too. Ellie could tell the kitchen hadn't been used for a few years, but it was *perfect*.

Whisk sneezed.

Well, maybe it was a little dusty!

Ellie brought out the magical recipe book, and put it on the worktop beside the cake while Victoria Sponge hovered above. To complete the *best friend* cake she needed butter, icing sugar and milk. Ellie went to the fridge and found some ingredients waiting for her, and a pot of icing sugar in the cupboard. They looked brand new!

"Victoria, how come these are here?" she asked. "Is this part of your magic?"

"Sorry. Did you say something?" the tiny cook replied, that same little smile on her face.

Ellie beat all the ingredients together, then tasted the mixture. It was really, really yummy, but she felt that there was still something missing. "How about vanilla essence?" she suggested. "It's not in the recipe, but . . ." She paused, suddenly worried that she might spoil the mix. "Or is that a stupid idea?"

"That's a *brilliant* idea, Ellie," said Victoria Sponge.

Ellie found some vanilla essence in a cupboard and added a couple of drops, mixing it in.

"Have you thought about how you'll decorate the cake?" Victoria Sponge asked.

85

Ellie nodded. She had the perfect design in mind!

Ellie arrived at the village green, with Whisk padding alongside her. The big white bake-off tent was packed full.

"Amazing!" she exclaimed.

There were so many brightly-decorated cakes and pastries and biscuits that the village green seemed greener. Even the presence of the grumpy-looking Scrudges couldn't spoil it. They looked ruffled and scruffy like they'd got there in a rush.

Suddenly Ellie spotted Basil. He was standing behind a table, a delicious-looking cake in front of him, and he was  wearing a T-shirt with a turtle on it. Ellie ran over with her cake tin, the magical recipe book tucked under her arm, Victoria Sponge hidden inside.

Whisk miaowed a hello and Basil stroked his head.

"I thought you said you weren't entering the bake-off?" Ellie asked, panting.

"I am now," he said. "Everyone is."

Basil pointed out Mr Amrit and some other villagers, who were all displaying cakes and tarts and other treats.

"But I thought people were too afraid of the Scrudges to enter," said Ellie.

"I spoke to Mr Amrit, who spoke to his friends, who spoke to their friends . . . We realized you were right, Ellie."

Ellie had no idea what she was right about.

"If everyone sticks together, we can be brave," Basil explained.

Ellie was stunned.

What an amazing couple of days it had been!

"You don't mind, do you?" he asked.

"Of course not," she said. It didn't matter who won – even if it *was* the Scrudges . . . as long as they won fairly.

Basil moved his cake along to make space for Ellie's, while Whisk sat under the table.

The competition was about to begin.

Chapter 7

Ellie's cake was decorated to show the moment she'd met Victoria Sponge in the woods. She'd coloured the icing to look like grass, and Victoria Sponge had posed while Ellie made a marzipan model of her.

"Wowwee, it looks so lifelike," said Basil.

"Thanks!" Ellie smiled.

Basil's cake was covered in chocolate buttons. "Your cake looks irresistible."

It *was* irresistible: Basil kept sneaking a button or two off it.

They watched and waited as everyone from the village piled in. So many people had entered this year that they had to use

extra tables from the picnic area. The organizers had brought in fans to keep everyone cool.

The two judges – the mayor of Greyton and a woman named Camilla Vanilla, who was a famous baker on TV – started making their way along the rows of cakes.

There were cream cakes, and lemon cakes, and marble cakes, and brownies. Ellie planned to ask the contestants for the recipes so she could try baking them all.

But there was one table in the corner that everyone seemed to be avoiding: the Scrudges'. They had last year's medal displayed in front of them. Their cake was labelled *Mud Pie*.

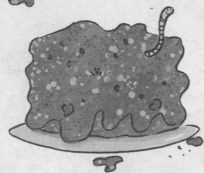

"It's actually made of mud," Ellie whispered to Basil.

Just then, a worm popped its head out of the middle of the pie.

Mr Scrudge quickly pulled it from the pie and passed it to Colin.

"Yuck," said Basil.

Ellie felt sorry for the judges who had to taste it. They were getting nearer, trying an apple crumble that looked delicious and even came with a jug of custard.

Colin approached Ellie's table with his fist tightly closed around something.

"Go away, Colin," Ellie told him.

"That's no way to speak to your biggers and betters," he said. He had a nasty look in his eye, and she knew from experience that he was about to do something mean.

Whisk hissed at him from under the table.

Colin opened his hand, and Ellie saw a pile of powdery earth on his palm. He lifted it to his lips.

"What are you . . . ?" But, too late, Ellie realized. He was going to blow mud all over her cake – making it just as muddy and disgusting as the Scrudges'!

"Isn't it hot in here?" Basil sighed dramatically. He had moved over to stand beside one of the fans.

Colin blew the earth onto Ellie's cake, just as Basil turned on the fan. The fan blew the earth back towards Colin.

His whole face was covered in it!

"Now who's stupid?" Basil said to Colin.

"Well, you . . . er – I mean, *are* . . . I . . . erm . . . Argh!" Colin ran off.

"Coward," said Basil.

Ellie giggled, and Basil gave her a high five.

"That showed *one* of the Scrudges," she said.

They looked over to where Mr and Mrs Scrudge were standing. The judges arrived at their table and their actual mud pie.

"This looks . . ." Camilla Vanilla's voice shook.

"I don't think I can eat this," said the mayor.

"You have to," said Mr Scrudge, shed-sized and towering over them. "It's the rules."

A woodlouse crawled across the top of the cake, leaving tracks all over the icing. The mayor went pale.

"He doesn't have to," said Mr Amrit, coming forward.

"Of course he doesn't," said the post-woman, standing beside him.

Ellie was glad to see the villagers finally standing up to the Scrudges. Together, they weren't afraid any more.

The mayor squared his shoulders and declared the Scrudges' cake a Health

Hazard. He wouldn't be eating it. Camilla
Vanilla took last year's medal from them
and continued down the line.

Mr Scrudge threw off his apron in anger.
Mrs Scrudge stamped her feet.

Ellie clapped. Finally the Scrudges were getting what they deserved!

The judges were now at Basil's table. They each took a large slice of Basil's chocolate cake and munched it.

"Yum," said the mayor.

"Lovely," agreed Camilla Vanilla.

"Wowweee! I'm so glad you like it," said Basil.

Ellie started to feel a bit nervous. She was next! She looked down for a final check on her cake, but — oh, no! Where was her marzipan Victoria Sponge?!

She searched around the table, moved Whisk out of the way so she could look

under him, but she couldn't see it anywhere.

"Lost something?" sneered Colin, who had crept up on the other side of her. He held the marzipan model of Victoria Sponge . . . and bit her head off!

What was Ellie going to do now? The judges were just making some final notes

on Basil's cake. They would be with her in seconds. With the model missing, her cake didn't look special enough. Maybe the Scrudges were right: maybe she was too small and too stupid to make cakes. Maybe she was too small and too stupid to do anything.

She was about to run out of the tent when the judges arrived.

"Have you got a name for your cake?" asked the mayor.

Ellie stuttered over her words. "It — it's called *A cake for a best friend*," she said. "I thought it was magical, but now . . ." She felt very silly.

103

"It looks amazing," said Camilla Vanilla.

"What a wonderful-looking marzipan figurine," the mayor commented.

"Huh?" Ellie looked down. The model was back in the centre of her cake, with its head in the right place.

"Very lifelike," said the mayor.

How did that happen? wondered Ellie.

As the two judges sliced into her cake, the model Victoria Sponge turned round and winked at her. It was Victoria Sponge – the *real* Victoria Sponge. She'd jumped out of the book and saved the day!

"What a delicious cake!" the mayor exclaimed.

"The vanilla essence in the icing is ingenious," Camilla Vanilla added.

The only thing left for Ellie to do was take a bite of her own cake — she'd been waiting for this! She cut a slice for Basil, and a small chunk for Whisk, and then a slice for herself. She closed her eyes before she bit into it, imagining what a magical cake might taste like.

As soon as it touched her mouth, her whole body was filled with wonderful sugary tingle. The creamy vanilla icing complemented the cake's spongy texture beautifully. Sweet, but not sickly.

It was *delicious*.

But would the magic recipe work? Would it find Ellie a best friend?

Chapter 8

All the bake-off contestants lined up beside the stage in the centre of the village green. Basil and Ellie stood next to each other and crossed their fingers. Whisk weaved in and out of their legs, which was his way of saying "Good luck!"

"We were glad to see so many entries in the competition this year," said Camilla Vanilla.

"Yes," the mayor agreed. "All the contestants did a great job . . ." He paused and looked at the Scrudges. "*Most* of the contestants did a great job," he corrected himself.

"But there can only be one winner," Camilla Vanilla said.

"Who do you think it will be?" Ellie whispered to Basil. "The postwoman made a very tangy key lime pie."

"And this year the bake-off winner is . . ."

"And Mr Amrit made a yummy-looking carrot cake," Basil whispered back.

". . . Ellie Simmonds!"

Ellie couldn't believe it. She'd won!

"Wowweee!" said Basil.

Ellie's smile took over her whole face as she walked up to the stage and received the gold medal.

Her cake was brought forward, Victoria Sponge still sitting on top. The magical baker winked again at Ellie so only she could see. Everyone clapped!

Ellie felt great. She wasn't too small, or too stupid. She could do anything!

"How do you feel, Ellie?" asked the mayor.

"I loved taking part," she replied. "Winning is . . . just the icing on the cake."

The villagers of Greyton cheered and whooped. Even through all the noise Ellie could hear Basil shout, "Well done, Ellie!" She couldn't remember when she had last felt this good, though there was something

that she still felt very sad about.

Suddenly Mr Scrudge stepped up on stage. He glared at the villagers and then at the judges. "You let her win because you felt sorry for her," he said.

"That's cheating," added Mrs Scrudge, puffing beside him.

"I'm taking this on grounds of unfair dismissal," said Mr Scrudge, and he yanked the medal from round Ellie's neck.

"Hey!" Basil shouted from the audience. A few of the other villagers joined in.

But Ellie was too downhearted to protest. She'd hoped that by eating her cake she would find a best friend. She'd tasted it. It was yummy, but the magic hadn't worked. Or maybe there was no such thing as magic after all.

"It's fine," Ellie told Basil as she climbed down from the stage. "Let them have it." She knew she'd won fair and square — and so did everybody else in the village.

That was all that mattered.

The Scrudges marched Ellie back to their bakery. "Straight to bed with you, Shrimp," Mrs Scrudge said. "You've done enough lying and cheating for one day."

Ellie didn't mind. She'd been awake  all night baking, and now she was exhausted. Besides, she was too sad to do anything but sleep. She picked up Whisk and nuzzled his fur as she walked upstairs to bed.

"You're a good cat," Ellie whispered to him. "But it's not the same as having a real best friend."

"Miaow," Whisk replied.

The cake had been her only hope. Now even that was gone.

The next morning Ellie was woken by the sound of people bustling about below her window.

She sighed. The Scrudges must have bullied everyone into coming to their bakery again. Nothing had changed.

She opened her window, and the first thing that hit her was the smell. It was yummy!

"Whisk, look!" she cried.

Whisk jumped up onto the windowsill. Down below, the whole village was lining up. Not for Scrudge's Bakery . . . but for the tiny little bakery at the end of the

high street.

"Come on!" Ellie
yelled. She threw on her clothes
and raced out of the house.

The queue of people outside the little
bakery went halfway up the road.
"What's everyone doing here?" Ellie
asked Mr Amrit, who was tenth in line.

"We're all desperate for a cake, Ellie!" he told her. "Camilla Vanilla told us just how delicious your baking was. Word spread, and now we all want to try some."

The crowds parted for Ellie and Whisk.

118

The boards on the shop had been taken down, the windows had been cleaned, and once she was inside, Ellie could feel the warmth from the ovens.

"Victoria Sponge!" she called. It must be the magical baker who had made this happen.

Victoria Sponge appeared from the larder. She was wearing her apron and

she had a smudge of flour on her nose. "Where have you been? We have so many orders for your bakery."

"*My* bakery?" asked Ellie.

"Of course!" she said. "Didn't you read your father's card?"

I've got a present for you, the card from Dad had said. "But he gave me the recipe book."

"Oh! I should have explained." Victoria hit herself on the head with her hand. "I got you the magical recipe book.

This bakery is the present from your father!"

Ellie was too amazed to speak.

"*Both* your parents were bakers. Your dad hoped you would one day become a baker too. He knew you would need a bakery that was just your size, and it's been waiting until you were old enough to use it." Victoria Sponge hovered closer to her ear. "He asked me to help because I'm a small cook, just like you."

Ellie didn't know how to run a bakery. She'd seen her dad do it right, and the Scrudges do it wrong, but could she manage her own? "It'll be a lot of hard work," she said.

"You've got me to help you," Victoria Sponge told her.

Ellie stopped being amazed and started being happy. She'd sell yummy cakes full of magical ingredients. She'd make it the best bakery in the world!

She found an apron on a low hook and hurriedly put it on. It was the perfect size – just as if it had been waiting for her to find it. The apron ties dangled down and

Whisk batted them playfully. It made Ellie
happy to think that her dad had planned
all this.

"I'm afraid it will take me a while to
make your orders," she told the people in
the queue.

123

"We'll help tidy while we wait." Camilla Vanilla, who was the first in line, rolled up her sleeves.

Ellie couldn't believe it — all these people pouring into her shop! They were dusting, mopping, cleaning, tidying. The postwoman had even brought brushes and paint.

"Couldn't you use magic to clean everything?" Ellie whispered to Victoria Sponge, thinking back to how she'd made the Scrudge's kitchen sparkle.

"Isn't it so much more fun this way?" said Victoria Sponge, looking around at all the people chatting as they lent a hand.

"Look what I've found," said the mayor. He held out a framed photograph and handed it to Ellie. 'Do you recognize him?'

Instantly Ellie was surrounded by the aroma of freshly baked cakes. The photograph showed her dad, with his ginger beard and round cheeks. He held a tray of cookies. And he was smiling at Victoria Sponge as she sprinkled her magical baking dust . . .

Her dad and Victoria Sponge *had* cooked together! Here was the photo to prove it.

"Wowweee," she muttered to herself.

Which made her think of Basil. She was surprised that he wasn't here with everybody else.

"Basil is outside," said Victoria Sponge,

as if reading her mind. "He was the first person to arrive this morning."

Ellie put down the photograph and ran out. Basil was up a ladder painting the sign above the shop. It read:

Ellie's Ma

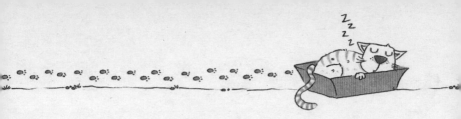

"Wowweee!" exclaimed Ellie.

"That's my line!" said Basil. And they both giggled.

"That looks amazing, Basil," she told him. "Thanks so much."

cal Bakery

Whisk had to jump out of the way as a drop of paint fell from Basil's brush. Basil had splatters of paint all over his caterpillar T-shirt.

'What are best friends for?' he asked.

Ellie gasped. The magic of the cake had worked after all! She had the best friend she had always wanted. And as she  looked around at all the people from Greyton helping out, she realized she had more than one friend in the village.

Greyton needed something to sweeten it up.

Ellie's Magical Bakery was just the place to do it.

Village Hall

POST OFFICE

SUPERMARKET

...ton High Street

SCRUDGE'S

Scrudge's Bakery

GREYTON

Hello, nice to meet you!

Do you like to bake?

Why don't you try out Ellie's recipe, and bake your own Best Cake for a Best Friend?

Make sure you **always** have a grown-up around to help.

When it's baked, you can decorate your cake in any way you like. Why don't you draw out some of your ideas?

Happy Baking!

Victoria Sponge

Best Cake for a Best Friend

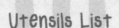

Cake Ingredients

100g softened butter, and some extra for greasing

100g caster sugar

2 eggs

100g self-raising flour (sifted)

2 – 3 tablespoons of jam

Icing Ingredients

100g butter

200g icing sugar (sifted)

2 tablespoonsful of cold milk, mixed with 0.5 – 1 teaspoonful of vanilla essence in a small cup

Food colouring (if you like)

Utensils List

Aprons

2 sandwich tins (18cm diameter)

Baking paper

Scissors

1 large bowl

1 wooden spoon

1 tablespoon / tbsp measurement

1 large metal spoon

Cooling rack

1 knife (for spreading)

1 small cup

1 medium-sized bowl

1 teaspoon / tsp measurement

1 spatula

Cake Recipe

1. Put your aprons on and preheat the oven to 180°C.

2. Line the tins with baking paper and grease the sides.

3. Cream the butter and sugar together in a large bowl until light and fluffy.

4. Beat in the eggs one at a time, adding a tablespoon of flour with each one.

5. Gently fold in the remaining flour using a metal spoon.

6. Divide the mixture equally between the tins and ask an adult to place them in the oven for 25 – 30 minutes.

7. When the sponges are ready, leave them to cool for 3 minutes, then turn them out onto a cooling rack.

8. When cool to the touch, sandwich the two sponges together with the jam plus a layer of icing.

Now you are ready to ice the top!

Icing Recipe

1. In a medium-sized bowl, beat the butter until soft, using a wooden spoon.

2. Gradually beat in the sugar alternatively with the milk/vanilla mix until your icing is light and fluffy.

3. If you like, add a few drops of food colouring!

4. Place the icing in the fridge for 30 minutes, to thicken.

5. Use some of the icing between the two cake layers and spread the rest over the top of the cake using a spatula.

Yum,
it's ready!

ELLIE SIMMONDS is a Paralympic swimming champion and has ten world records to her name. At 14, Ellie was the youngest recipient of the MBE, and also now has an OBE – both special titles awarded by the Queen. Ellie has continued to succeed in swimming, but she also loves to bake! Working on Ellie's Magical Bakery is a really exciting new way for Ellie to pursue her love of cakes and bakes.

Ellie's disability is called Achondroplasia (dwarfism). Achondroplasia means that Ellie has shorter arms and legs than most people. As a result Ellie is a lot smaller than other people her age, but this has never stopped her from doing the things she loves the most.

KIMBERLEY SCOTT is a professional illustrator and designer. She regularly works on a diverse range of projects and loves to delve into imaginative worlds. Kimberley lives and works in London, from her teeny-weeny studio, with a constant supply of green tea and pick-and-mix sweets to keep her creativity flowing!